Mehrdad Shahmoradi Mofrad has an artistic background. He studied in Vienna's Art School and attended some semesters at the Vienna's Film Academy as a guest student and later as a part-time student for a year.

Mehrdad Shahmoradi Mofrad

ENDLESS MISSION III

AUSTIN MACAULEY PUBLISHERS™

LONDON • CAMBRIDGE • NEW YORK • SHARJAH

A CIP catalogue record for this title is available from the British Library.

ISBN 9781035860500 (Paperback)
ISBN 9781035860517 (ePub e-book)

www.austinmacauley.com

First Published 2024
Austin Macauley Publishers Ltd®
1 Canada Square
Canary Wharf
London
E14 5AA

Table Of Content

London, England Forest
Near John's Flat

On a sunny autumnally day, John and Karen are walking on a winding walkway. The leaves have formed a bridge grown from the boughs crossing over one another from the trees of both sides and assemble a tunnel like construct in their beneath whilst the walkway continues into the forest.

They stop, they kiss one another.

She starts slowly to go for jogging and distances herself from John whilst he continues to walk.

He does not notice the oncoming cyclist but hears pedalling of a bicycle, as he turns to the left to see who is coming, the cyclist hits John on his hip.

John falls on the ground, sees a booklet with an inscription, "Journal," laying on the pathway near to him.

As soon as he wants to pick it up, the same cyclist is riding back with speed and is looking back over the shoulder in direction of the another sitting who seems to be an older person.

John is still laying on the walkway and turns himself to a side, out of the walkway on the grass laying aside, to prevent himself from being hit again by the cyclist. The cyclist stops, stretches the right arm, tries to get the booklet from John. She can take it and hold it for a fleeting time to tear up some pages out of it.

John pushes back the cyclist's arm. Someone whistles. The cyclist drops down the booklet on the walkway and rides quickly away.

John who does not seem to have heard the whistling, looks again at the journal, as it is now within his reach and stretches out his right arm, reaches for the journal and holds it in his right hand's fingers.

Still laying on the ground, he looks to see if he can locate the cyclist who by now has vanished through the forest.

He looks around to see if anyone else has been witnessing this accident, noticing him or the cyclist.

He stands up, walks towards the bench nearby and sits on it.

On another bench far away to this one, sits the older person whom the cyclist was looking at over the shoulder.

John looks towards that person, looks back at the journal, and feels less oriented.

He leans back on the bench, breathes deep in and out, begins to look closer into this finding and with an excited voice, says: "This handwriting, I recognise it! It is Slyer's!?"

He opens the Journal, looks through the pages and says: "These are set in session or rather scenes without being numbered, like an agenda for what is to be done or to be expected."

He begins to read from the open page:

"In order to have an overview, I structure my journal by setting it into scenes without numbering them, in form of a theatrical draft. They shall follow one another, like Samuel's way of working:

Scene

"I couldn't find out how the gas was on its way from the laboratory to the front, so I sent agent Pinter."

John stops reading and says: "Indeed, Pinter."

He turns some pages forward and continues reading:

Scene

"Judd's deployment seemed to be an alternative but at the end each and every one of our efforts to halt the chlorine gas from further production and usage is failing bitterly deadly."

He turns some pages forward and continues to read:

Scene

"The stick of dynamite and the shadow on kitchen's window. I did not put the dynamite stick in the box, but the shadow on the window, had gone shortly before I left the kitchen and only had seen the stick and the box. Probably adding one and one together, would have thought: The dynamite is in the box.

I put it back in the shelf before leaving the kitchen and after I was certain of the shadow's disappearance.

John hears a voice coming from behind saying:

"We could call it a history, the one we made."

John tunes himself around, sees a man looking at him smiling, using a small spray in his left hand, pressing its small ball to spray out at the same time a breeze blows the sprayed back to him whilst he continues saying: "You are still on duty."

John smiles and says: "It is you, dear general!"

Slyer: "General was my rank that left me in with the endless missions."

John: "What was that you sprayed out?"

Slyer: "Oh, that spraying, it is just to clean the air. I am allergic to this sort of fresh air coming out of a forest."

John isn't sure if this man is the real Slyer, something in his voice makes John doubtful, he asks: "How did you know about this walkway, where I usually go for a walk?"

Slyer: "Just coincidently. Of course, I knew that you live nearby."

John: "There are reasons to assume that the mission is not yet accomplished."

Slyer: "You are still adamant... Tell me... State your case, the reasons for it."

John: "One reason; the chemist is dead; he is not dead. We simply do not know, furthermore whether or not he is still experimenting on producing other chemicals based on his chlorine gas, to be even worse than the first one!"

Slyer: "Everything has an end."

John: "Will he give up by whatever else he might be producing?"

Slyer: "You mean only a dead chemist is a good chemist?"

John: "In his case, it might be!"

Slyer: "There will be others, from all other different armies."

John: "Yes!"

Slyer is moving himself closer to John and John is still not sure whether or not this man indeed, is Slyer, for one reason, Slyer is trying to get a better view to have a look at the journal that is on the bench next to him.

John realises this, picks up the journal and holds it in his right hand whilst Slyer has been following these movements and asks with sudden attack of coughing:

"That booklet, it looks familiar, let me see, how did you come in its possession?"

Slyer coughs again and after some seconds John who is still suffering slightly from his crash with the cyclist a while ago, seems to see Slyer with a different deformed face.

He closes his eyes, rubs them, and opens them again.

Slyer: "Aren't you feeling well? You seem to be becoming out of your breath. And your eyes, they seem to be becoming redder…"

John: "No, I am fine. How about you?"

Slyer: "I merely coughed."

John: "Just for a moment though, I thought, you weren't… Never mind."

Slyer sneezes and seems to be adjusting his chin with his right hand, to the right and to the left and then in the middle again.

John is weary and is watching Slyer.

Slyer sneezes once more and says: "Your head seems to be spinning around your neck, isn't it?"

John: "Is it visible?"

Slyer: "Yes, so much like I am visible to you."

John remains silent whilst he is still looking at Slyer, says: "Dismally I see you; but your face looks like a melting rubber. I do not recognise you as the real general."

Slyer: "Even the generals degenerate with time."

John: "And becoming who?" whilst he is becoming more and more out of breath.

Slyer: "Degenerated generals, of course. Not the ones they used to be."

John: "You found a friend in an enemy?"

Slyer looks at journal John is still holding in his right hand and says: "You mean the Germans; they found a friend in me to my agony."

John: "Or that of the enemy's?"

Slyer: "Even as!"

He looks sceptically at Slyer and puts back the journal on his left side.

Slyer continues: "Counterparts, as Deborah, you remember my wife, used to call them and as such introduced them to me…"

John: "To your resentment?"

Slyer: "At the beginning, yes, and to some extent my curiosity kept me from rejecting them. After some time, I thought to have made some progress by involving them more and more in fighting against their own gas production but after all that, what had happened to my staff, I lost the overview and exactly then they departed from us and went back to Germany, leaving me with an empty box of pralines."

John: "What happened to that stick of dynamite?"

Slyer: "Stick of dynamite?!"

John: "You know: the dynamite."

Slyer: "Oh yes, I recall. I didn't use it."

John: "And the shadow on the window?"

Slyer: "I couldn't identify it either."

John's suspicion is becoming more concrete, but he doesn't act upon it yet and asks: "But you had it with you, the dynamite I mean, at the meeting, hadn't you?"

Slyer: "Yes."

John: "You were cautious."

Slyer: "Yes."

John is now certain that the man sitting next to him on the bench cannot be Slyer. He looks to the further away sitting older person, who is standing up and is starting to walk towards their direction.

He looks back at Slyer and is confronted with a pistol pointed at him, Slyer says: "I am not Slyer, hand me that booklet!"

John says: "Shadow I presume!?"

Fake Slyer: "No."

John picks up the journal and throw it in front of him on the ground.

Fake Slyer: "This is a very old trick. Stand up, pick it up and hand it to me!"

John: "You are not Slyer, and you are not the shadow on the window. Tell me: who are you then?"

Meanwhile the older person is getting nearer.

The fake Slyer: "Someone who does not exist but to be fair with you, one of the old counterparts."

John notices the coming nearer of the older person, picks up the journal, turns and stands in front of the fake Slyer, blocking his view to the coming person. He gives him the journal.

The fake Slyer: "Thank you," whilst keeping the pistol towards John and is about to put his finger on the trigger… A voice comes from behind, shouting: "Throw yourself on the ground, John."

John throws himself on the ground and a shot is discharged, the fake Slyer falls on the ground in front of him.

John stands up, turns himself to the older person and sees an elderly woman and asks: "Who are you?"

Elder woman: "No time to ask, check to see if he is still alive!"

He bows to the laying man, turns him, facing him frontal, sees a partially scratched mask that has come off the fake Slyer's face, and is still weakly breathing. He pulls the mask slowly away from the fake Slyer's face.

The old person: "Do you know this man, have you seen him before?"

John pauses and says: "How about you, do you happen to know or recognise him? Just a moment; your voice of course, you are Deborah. Who else would have remembered those lifesaving words:

"Throw yourself."

Deborah: "Yes, still remembering them since our mission begun. And now after all those years, almost over twenty years, I had to use them again, just in time to save and sadly to kill.

"Dear John, we are still facing the same enemy and its same threats."

John: "Let's with speed to hospital before this man dies!"

London
A Military Hospital

Deborah and John are waiting in the corridor outside of the surgery room.

John: "I don't know where to start from. We lost sight of each other."

Deborah is looking at John silently as John continues:

"Where is General Paul Slyer?"

Deborah: "He died."

John: "Died? How, when?"

Deborah: "Two years ago. He had a stroke."

John: "And Simon Joyful?"

Deborah: "He attended the funeral and told me that he was about to travel to the continent."

John: "To the continent? I might find him there if I were looking for him?"

Deborah: "Yes, if you were."

John: "I am beginning to think about the past and to today's encountering. Did he tell you where he was going to, exactly?"

Deborah: "I am afraid not. You are still so persistent, aren't you?"

John: "Yes, but I don't want to be annoying, thou… Did you happen to notice what happened here on the walkway prior to the shooting?"

Deborah: "From afar, not much but of course I saw him getting closer to you."

John: "So, who is this man really? He told me to be one of the counterparts, you might be able to identify him, since you knew all or most of them."

Deborah: "He is the one who telephoned me."

John: "Telephoned you? You never mentioned. Was he an agent, a German agent? I know that you use to have informers or rather double agents working for you and your department."

Deborah: "Yes, in the nineteenth fourteens, it was everybody's double game till, after some years, when all of a sudden, the murdering of Judd was committed by using or trying to hire them.

"I hardly sighted the double agents from close to me, rather contacting them either by letter or by telephone."

John: "Confusing."

Deborah: "Puzzling, indeed."

John looks suspiciously at Deborah; she realises this and says:

"I know that look; you had been working very closely to Paul and might have had it inherited."

John: "Oh, I am sorry."

At the same time the surgeon comes out of the surgery and says: "He died; I am afraid, we could not do anything more but before he died, he was able to whisper some words…"

John: "What words?"

Surgeon: "The journal, it must be destroyed…!"

She and John look to one another, John asks: "The journal?"

Surgeon: "Yes. The reddening of his nose. I hadn't seen such a one before. And of course, the mask. Was he also a clown, by any chance? Do you know how his flush…?"

John: "The flush? He used a spray."

Dr: "A spray? What was its content?"

John: "We analysed it and found a sprayable toxic. He said that he needed it for his allergy that he had from the fresh air coming out of the forest. It must have been blown back to him. I was exposed also to it, but it was too little to have an effect on me. I was hit by bicycle rider before, and I was dizzy for some time."

Dr: "Agents and their spying games!"

He leaves them and goes back to his ward.

Deborah: "The journal, but of course."

John: "What were you there for?"

Deborah: "I knew you occasionally walk there, and I wanted to see and talk to you."

John: "What about?

Deborah: "I was wondering, if your eyes are still locked on that red ribboned archived file?"

John: "Actually, I was about to unlock my eyes and start anew but now, it depends."

Deborah: "On what?"

John: "On your eyes and mind!"

Deborah: "Yes, the missions are still on my mind, as if it were yesterday. By the way, I did not know Paul was keeping a journaling."

John: "Neither did I. It seems as if I interrupted a handing over! We might find answers in the journal."

Deborah: "The cyclist! We must remain vigilant. Can you remember any details on the bicycle or on the person who was riding it?"

John breaths deep in and out and says: "The person had a cap on, man or a woman, not visible.

The bicycle, I guess, with that speed, it must have been a "Sun Wasp lightweight…"

Deborah: "There aren't many of them."

They look at one another and Deborah says: "Let us look into the journal."

John's Flat

John and Deborah are sitting in the sitting room and having afternoon tea.

John: "The finding of the journal and the clash."

Deborah: "I am not sure, but I think, Paul wrote more than he told us."

John: "Maybe he didn't want us to get more involved due to lacking the verified information."

John opens the journal and starts reading:

Scene

"I was informed of the chemist sojourn in England. I was given the information about his rapid sickening and where he was travelling to, namely to Switzerland.

I forwarded this information to my agents for foreign missions to come back to London and localise him, since he had British sympathisers who might help him for blocking my homebased agents to follow his streps to Switzerland that would be his next destination.

Furthermore, I did not want to involve Deborah, John, or Simon, because they were under tremendous strain and known to them." John stops reading.

Deborah: "Continue, please."

John looks at the journal, turns some pages forward, he senses with the tip of his fingers the rests of some pages that had been torn and cut out.

He looks at Deborah and says: "There is no more to read from," without mentioning the missing pages.

They look at one another and Deborah says: "Should we to Switzerland or remain here and operate further?"

John: "Operate furthermore? I am retired, you are not at

that age for an another... I am sorry, you are also in retirement, but I must say, still a good shooter thou. But aren't we older now for yet another mission?"

Deborah: "Older, matured, and still armed. I could activate some of the double agents..."

John interrupts her and says: "They are probably dead by now if their chieves haven't killed them already after uncovering their double activities."

Deborah: "It is worth a try, won't you admit? Besides we owe it to the rest of us who failed with us."

John takes a deep breath in and out saying: "Alright, what are our options... Resources?"

Deborah: "Who was that woman with you in the park?"

John: "Karen Balt, you know her, remember?"

Deborah: "Dr Karen Balt? Yes, but I hardly worked with her. How long do you know her, apart from your therapy with her in the past?"

John remains silent.

Deborah pauses and says: "You love her?" She notices a wedding ring on John's ring finger and holds her breath for a second, breaths out but doesn't show her noticing of the ring.

John: "Neither have you lost your surveillance sense, nor that of your interrogation's skills."

Deborah: "Is she still your therapist?"

John remains silent for some seconds, closes his eyes, and says: "A helpful friendship. We are married."

Deborah: "You can trust her?"

John: "Of course I can, and you should, too. Remember she used to work for military services."

Deborah remains silent and after some seconds says: "I guess, we should get out of age and become active again. You shall ask her to help us."

John nods positively and says: "I'll find out about that bicycle. But tell me, did you put the journal on the walkway, for me to find it?"

Deborah: "Yes. You were the closer one to Paul's working world. I was only his wife and a distanced colleague. To see, if you were alone and still in that world, I chose to find out by doing so and to bring you into my mine."

John looks at her and realises the importance of what she said and did, says: "Thank you for letting me into your world. We will pursue!"

Deborah's Flat

Deborah, Karen, and John are sitting in the living room.

Deborah: "Let us find the chemist."

Karen asks: "How many times have you two have said this sentence and then? These missions have not been of any success but full of casualties, deadly ones."

John: "We owe a conclusion to those casualties."

Karen: "You include yourself, too, don't you? Will the dead soldiers from all sides rise up and come out of their graves?"

Deborah: "How about securing the future? A conclusion shall serve the future security."

John: "I agree, nevertheless there is not a constant secure world rather an ever changing one. How about you Doctor, what is your opinion?"

Karen nodes positively and asks: "Since you ask me with my medical degree, I ask; When shall we start?"

Deborah: "We start with possible accomplices who might still be operating here in London or Liverpool."

John: "Are there some left?"

Deborah bows her head slightly and answers: "I can check."

Karen: "Once you locate any of them, I shall start my work."

John: "And it would be!?"

Karen: "Talk to them of course." She smiles at John and afterwards at Deborah.

John: "But of course."

Deborah: "John, you shot one after he ran out of the Chelsea flat. I shot another one who claimed to you to be one of the counterparts who took part on those meetings. It is important to know if there are anyone left from those who attended the meetings and talk to them."

John: "I am overwhelmed, ladies, our strategy is colouring!"

Karen: "Apart from the dead one now, the cyclist might have some answers. How about finding him or she?"

John: "I couldn't tell the difference."

Deborah stands up and goes to her study. John and Karen look at one another and remain in the living room where they hear sounds of opening and shutting of draws and after some minutes are getting rarer and stop.

Deborah comes out of her study with a rather,

thicker file, puts it on the table before Karen and John.

She opens the file, Karen and John join her at the table. She takes some photographs out of the file, shows them, and says: "These two were amongst the counterparts at the meetings Paul and I had with them. The one shot by me was also a part of them. So, I gather, if I get in touch with the rest…"

Karen says: "After studying your files, rather not. I was for involving the rest but this time, it must be under absolute secrecy."

Deborah looks at John as he says: "She is right. It is better not to involve anybody else."

Karen and John look at Deborah. Deborah nods positively and smiles.

John: "I could get some information about that bicycle; it was bought from a shop at Edgware Road. The buyer was a woman."

Deborah: "A woman? Did you see a woman on that bicycle who was running you over?"

John: "I couldn't because she had a cap on…"

Karen: "Probably to cover her hair with."

Deborah: "We cannot be sure. Let us do some observation on the Edgware Road. She may live near that shop."

Edgware Road

Deborah and Karen are sitting at the table, inside a café on the Edgware Road opposite the bicycle shop. They are having tea and cakes.

Karen: "I wonder why you are still so concerned about the chemist. You nor John need any avower for unsuccessful missions mostly due to sabotage by double-crossing agents."

Deborah: "No, but to see the end to this long mission, it would be a well-served gratification, personally and not less a triumph."

Karen looks across the street and sees a woman who goes in that shop and fetches a bicycle."

Karen looks at Deborah and turns her head to Deborah and then towards the woman. Deborah also does the same and says: "Yes."

Karen: "So be it a woman:"

Deborah: "We shadow her."

The woman begins to walk away from the shop. She is rolling her bike with her right hand.

Deborah and Karen follow some seconds afterwards.

The woman goes along the shops and turns into the next alley to the left and continues walking whilst Deborah and Karen are still following her.

They stop as the woman stops in front of a house on her right side and gets a key out of her purse, opens the front door, and enters the house.

They get closer to the house and look up the facete and see a light shines out of the window on the third floor of the house.

They see a restaurant obliquely across, go inside, sit at a table, and look up the menu card, order some food and drinks.

After some time, the woman comes out of the house and starts to walk away.

At the same time John who had been also following Karen and Deborah to keep watch out for them, is waiting outside of the restaurant, follows the woman without letting himself to be seen by Karen or the woman nor by Deborah.

Deborah and Karen pay the bill, get out of the restaurant, and go to that house.

Deborah opens the lock, with tools which she had taken out of her purse whilst Karen had been watching her astounded.

They enter the house, climb the stairs to the third floor and look through the corridor's window to the left and to the right to locate the window of the apartment through the one, the light shined.

Deborah opens the door of the apartment, they could locate, and enter in, see some photographs and papers on the table in the study.

Karen goes to the room next to the study; Deborah picks up some of photographs and sees Paul and herself pictured in some of photographs on different occasions.

She looks further through the papers, Karen comes out of the room, passes by Deborah who is still turning the pages of the papers and goes to the kitchen, comes back to Deborah, and asks: "Find anything?"

Deborah: "Here, look at the photographs, and these cut out pages, they seem to be at the same size as the ones of the journal's. By looking closer, I determine Paul's handwriting. Look they are written like a play, scenes, following one another but not numbered. I wonder why, John didn't tell me about any missing pages?"

Karen: "Maybe he did not find any traces. But never mind that now, we have some new material to investigate. How about that woman? Must we deal with her?"

Deborah: "Let me think… No, we'd better deliver her to the police by giving the police some anonymous hints about a foreign agent activity."

Karen: "Don't you think that she might have more information about the chemist?"

Deborah: "I do not think so. But we shall wait before having her known by the police."

Karen: "You don't really want to take those pages with you?"

Deborah: "No, we leave everything as it is. Go and keep a watch on the window to see if she is coming back. I will write off every page."

In the meantime, in a narrow alley near to the woman's place, John is observing from afar the woman and a younger man talking to one another.

The young man leaves her, John goes to her, blocks her way, and asks: "Tell me who you are, who was the young man!?"

She remains calm as John continues: "My name is John Barr. You were riding a bicycle, remember? On the walkway into the forest?"

She: "My name is Monica Ulrich."

John: "Monica, what was it you wanted on the walkway?"

Monica: "You'd better tell me!"

John: "What do you mean?"

Monica: "The booklet, it was meant for you. I had seen the old person before you came. She put it there on the ground, and I wanted to take it before you might have found it."

John asks: "A booklet for me? With whom do you work? Who was that man after you left the walkway?"

Monica: "I come from Germany. I live and study here in London, to earn my living I work with the German foreign intelligence services as a freelance agent."

John: "Why are you telling me all these?"

Monica: "I have nothing to hide. Besides I feel sorry to have hit you. You might help me finding someone, someone important to me as well as to you!"

John: "You can tell me more about it and about their activities, can't you"

Monica: "I am not sure; I am following you!"

John: "I mean to work for them as well as for us."

Monica: "Is such a thing possible?

John smiles, nods positively and asks: "How did you become aware of me?"

Monica: "I found your files in the office."

John: "Office, do they still keep old files?"

Monica: "They were aware of your possible encounter with the fake Slyer."

John remains silent. They leave the alley as John says:

"Do not go home, yet. Can I meet with that young man, you were talking to?"

Monica nods positively.

Deborah's Flat

Deborah, Karen, and John are sitting at a round table in the study and are looking into the written pages from the Monica's place.

Deborah looks at John and says: "You did notice the cut-out pages from the journal, didn't you?"

John: "Yes."

Deborah is still looking at him…

John continues: "… I did not want to worry you unnecessarily. That woman, I talked to her, to that woman."

Karen: "What do you mean? You talked to her, during or before we were at her place?"

John interrupts her and asks: "Did she really have the cut-out pages?"

Deborah: "Yes, as you can see."

John: "And have you read them?"

Karen: "Deborah wrote off the pages while we were there. We left the place as it was. You were supposed to look after us."

John: "Of course, you didn't notice me, but I was there."

Deborah: "Let us not to lose time and start to read the pages."

John interrupts her and says: "Not curious about my accidental meeting with her?"

Karen and Deborah look at him.

John: "Her Name is Monica Ulrich; she is a German student who is living and studying here in London. Now don't be surprised as I continue saying that she works with the German Foreign Intelligence to finance herself."

Karen and Deborah look at one another and then at him.

John takes a breath in and let it out and continues: "After she left her place, I followed her, and I could talk to her in an alley nearby during your search of her place."

Deborah: "We should talk to her. John, you organise it. I have the first page. It seems to be the beginning of them, it says—"

John interrupts her and says: "Deborah, I would like to have a word with you, please."

Karen: "That is a good idea I will go and make some tea," and leaves the room.

John: "That woman is either very naive or she has a scheme."

Deborah: "What do you mean?"

John: "She started to tell me everything, about the walkway accident and the journal, saying it was already laying there. She had been observing you, too. Did you not notice her?"

Deborah: "I did, and waited to see till you notice, find the booklet."

At the same time Karen steps into the room with a Tablet of a teapot and cups, saying: "Tea and biscuits."

John: "I will introduce you to her who strangely enough, might become an asset."

Karin looks at Deborah.

Karen: "She might be helpful after all. Didn't she tell you at the end, her purpose of getting involved in this mission with you?"

John: "She said that we were looking for an important person because of his importance to both of us."

Karen: "I wonder, what she meant by that."

Deborah: "It is strange, indeed!"

Monica's Flat

John, Karen, Deborah, and Monica are sitting in the drawing room.

Deborah is looking at Monica and says: "We want to find the chemist."

Karen is looking at Monica and says: "You know of course whom we are talking about! Might you be an acquaintance of him?" stops speaking and smiles.

Monica is silently looking at her and asks: "And?"

John and Deborah look at Karen questionably.

As she continues: "You told John that you were a student here and that you were working with the German Foreign Intelligence Services…"

Monica interrupts her and says: "Yes, but I have not a high-level rank, just a freelance contractor."

Deborah: "We read from the torn-out pages saying that the chemist might be in Switzerland, have you any knowledge of that?"

Monica: "No, how could I?"

Karen: "You could find out, thou. Just use the information available at their office."

Deborah: "But be cautious!"

John: "Isn't that important person the chemist?"

While the others are looking at her, Monica answers:

"He might be."

Dr Karen Balt's Office

Karen is sitting at her desk. She is thinking about what Monica meant by saying those words to John: "A person, important to both of us. He might be."

There is an open file in front of her. she turns some pages, stops, picks up the telephone receiver, dials the telephone operator and asks: "Connect me, please, to the psychiatric hospital in Berlin, Germany. Ask for Dr Georg Markus."

After some minutes the operator rings back and says:

"Dr Balt, you can speak with Dr Markus, now."

Karen: "Doktor Markus, hier spricht Doktor Balt aus London, Sie erinnern mich?"

"(Doctor. Markus here is Dr Balt speaking from London. You remember me.")

Markus: "Ja, Dr Balt, ich erinnere mich an Sie, was kann ich für Sie tun?"

(Yes. Dr Balt I remember you. What can I do for you?")

Balt: "Ich brauche einige Informationen über den Chemist."

(Dr Balt: "I need, some information about the chemist.)"

Doktor. Markus: "Sie geben nicht auf, Frau Doktor Balt, hartnäckig wie immer, wie Sie während Ihrer Zeit als meine

Studentin auf der Universität waren. Der Mann ist wahrscheinlich bereits Tod. Was wollen Sie noch von ihm?"

(Dr Markus: "You won't give up Dr Balt, stubborn as usual, during your time as my student at the university. The man is probably already dead. What do you still want from him?")

Karen: "Hätte er dieses teuflische Gas aufgegeben, hätten wir dieses Telefonat nicht durchführen müssen. Stimmen Sie nicht mit mir?)

(Karen: "If he had given up this devilish gas, we wouldn't have had to have this telephony! Wouldn't you agree?")

Dr Markus: "Sie sind immer noch die, die das letzte Wort haben muss!"

(You are still the one who must have the last word.")

Doktor Markus: "Was wollen Sie noch über ihm Wissen?"

(What more do you want to know about him?"

Karen: "Familienstand, Kinder."

(Familiare. Wife, Children.)"

Doktor Markus: "Ehefrau, Tod, Kinder: zwei, einen Sohn und eine Tochter."

"(Dr Markus: „Wife dead, Children: a son and a daughter.)"

Balt: "Danke, Doktor."

(Thank you, doctor.)

Doktor. Markus: "Wir sollten die Vergangenheit auf sich berühren lassen."

(Doctor. Markus: "We should let the past touch us.")

Karen puts the receiver down, holds her head, closes her eyes. She opens her eyes and looks through the files in front of her.

She takes some photographs out of one of the files, takes a magnifier out of a drawer in her desk, looks closer to one of them, finds a metal container, puts the photograph back.

She concentrates herself, looks into the other photographs in front of herself.

A reflection of a "World War I", scenery begins to be shimmering in her eyes, she views:

A metal container, two hands that are holding and laying it on the table. It is being wrapped and packaged without any markings on it.

Afterwards it is being put in a small military van, at the laboratory's rear gate.

The door is being closed, the van is driven away and is passing by some hills. It reaches an airbase. It stops, the driver gets off the van, goes to the back of the van, opens the back door, takes out the package and goes toward the plane, and is now by a small plane with running engines, awaiting him,

He opens the plane's door and puts the package in the hands of another person who takes it and closes the door.

The driver distances himself from the plane, observes the plane's taking off and its fading into the sky. He gets back to the van, gets in, and drives away.

She hears a knock on the door but doesn't reply. She thinks to hear it out of her viewing and continues viewing:

The plane fades in, out of the sky and sets to landing on air base surrounded by barb wire and trees for an adequate hideout.

One more knock on the door and a voice is heard from outside saying: "Karen, it is me, may I come in?"

After a short pause, Karen answers: "Yes."

John: "Didn't you hear my knocking at the door?

Karen: "I was sorting out my files, I am behind some of my schedules."

John: "Can I help you?"

Karen: "Look in my eyes. Can you see any reflection, in my eyes, apart from yours?"

John: "Let me have a look. There is only mine and the rest behind me."

Karen: "I spoke to my old professor in Germany…"

John: "I didn't know that you were still in touch with him."

Karen: "I wasn't, till after being introduced to Monica."

John: "Yes, it is very curious, indeed!"

Karen: "How do you mean?"

John: "She was very candid with me. I started a conversation and she even apologised for her hitting me with the bicycle and telling me about her spying job."

Karen: "I call my old professor and asked him about the chemist's familiar."

John: "The chemist's familiar?"

Karen: "Yes."

John: "We forgot to elicit his familiar?"

Karen: "Perhaps, it was not very important at that stage of the investigation. He has a son and a daughter. He had a wife who died, committed suicide, that is, and this young woman might be…"

John: "I thought, we had proper and a thorough check of the chemist but… And how about the son? Do you think we could find him, too? Just a moment… She was talking to a young man in the alley during my observation of her."

Karen: "Do you think, what I think?"

John: "I do. How old might they be by now? Are they seeking their lost parents? Do they know about their mother's or their father's fate?"

Karen: "Let us put this aside for now and concentrate on how we ensure their trust towards us."

John nods positively.

Karen stands up, get closer to John, puts her hands around his neck and kisses him."

John: "Are you sure I can leave you now?"

Karen: "Yes, of course."

John leaves her office, Karen goes back to her desk, sits at her desk, and looks again to the pile of files. Slowly she slides them aside, takes a pocket mirror out of her purse to see if there are any shimmering in her eyes, or any reflections are coming back into them.

She looks in the mirror, the shimmering sets in her eyes and she views anew a flow of the pictorials:

The plane has landed on the airfield near the front, the pilot gets off the plane and goes to the back of the plane opens the cargo door, takes the metal container out, hands it to the soldier standing next to him who takes the metal container, carries it to the vehicle standing by and puts it on the seat next to that of the driver's, sits on the driver's place, ignites the vehicle, and drives away from the airfield.

She hears a knocking at the door again, this time distinctly, and says: "Come in."

John enters as Karen asks: "Forgot anything?"

John: "How about a break? Let's go to my place."

She takes her purse, puts back the mirror and one of the files inside it. They leave her office.

John's Flat

Karen and John are having supper, John says: "The file! How about the shimmering in your eyes, are they related to one another?"

Karen: "You saw them, too?"

John: "Yes, let us see where they might lead us to."

Karen: "I viewed a metal container without markings on it…"

John is looking through the file on the table next to his dish, says: "Like this one in this photograph?"

Karen: "Yes."

John: "Continue."

Karen: "It was transported on a van, then on an aeroplane. It landed on an airfield near a front…"

John: "Which front?"

Karen: "I couldn't follow up, you knocked on my door and invited me to this supper, in process of getting cold…"

John: "Oh, I am sorry, you are right. Afterwards we could continue."

Karen: "Or?" She takes John's hand and looks in his eyes."

John smiles and kisses her hand. They finish the diner.

In the Bedroom

They are laying on the bed and keeping each other in one another's arm.

John says: "Can we proceed?"

Karen looks at him and smiles.

John: "I mean with the file and…!"

Karen says: "Yes."

John: "Can the metal container be the very first, the original, carrying the chlorine gas to the front? This photograph must be from the WWI. We should travel as tourists to Switzerland. I always wanted to travel to Switzerland. You would rather mobilise his children and I the Deborah."

Karen nods positively.

John remains silent for the moment and is about to ask as Karen asks: "How can we persuade the children to come with us to Switzerland?"

John: "Monica is the one who might help the persuasion."

Karen: "What is his, the young man's name?"

John: "It is getting hard for me to keep up with all these questions and looking for answers. We even have to create answers for our own questions. We should, no, I would say: we must forget this endlessness. Who cares anyway? You have brilliantly connected the details of these photographs together like an animation."

Karen: "Hold my hand!"

John holds her hand.

Karen continues: "These photographs, they are not from WWI."

John: "What do you mean?"

Karen: "They were taken about a year ago."

John: "A year ago? How did it come into your possession?"

Karen: "Last year I attended a seminar in Minsk, you remember."

John nods positively and Karen continues: "and I was acquainted with Sergei Dalvik, a Russian journalist. He told me that he was on his way from Switzerland to Poland via Germany. It can only be the German border with Poland."

John: "Then we are going to the wrong country."

Karen: "No, Switzerland is the right one. We will find the chemist, if he is still alive and with the help of his children, we convince him not to use or let the chlorine gas be used again in whichever likely war to come."

John: "Do you know what you are saying? Oh, no, I am sorry. There is a chance, with help of his children, all very vague. It is out of his hands. It is and was in those of the German military's."

Karen: "He only needs to say: the gas is useless because there are adequate number of protective measures to advert the gas. Furthermore, the gas is about to be prohibited internationally."

John: "A bluff, that even seems to be convincing to you!"

Karen: "Yes."

Monica's Flat

John, Karen, Deborah, Monica, and a young man are sitting in the sitting room.

Monica: "This is my brother; George Wolff. On Karen's request I asked him to join us and listen to what you have to say. So, Karen, please tell him what you want from him and also from me!?"

Karen remains silent and Deborah says: "We are wondering, if both of you are aware of your father's work?"

Monica and George look at each. Monica asks: "Our father?"

George: "Our father, the gas?"

John looks at Deborah and then at Karen.

Karen: "We are in haste, and I must add, we are in danger, all of us, that includes you two as well."

John: "What you can do is, to tell us or to go with us, if you in knowledge of knowing, where in Switzerland he might live. We have to pursue with our mission and find him."

George: "What for? I mean the gas was spread; the war ended. What else can he do?"

Monica: "The last we heard about him was that he was sick."

Deborah: "Whom from?"

George: "What do you mean: whom from?"

Monica: "What a difference would it make? From a friend of a friend and so on."

John: "And you weren't curious at all, to go to him and to care for him?"

George and Monica look at one another and Monica answers:

"Care for him? Did he care for any of us or for the killings of the others?"

Karen realises that the siblings' emotions are very existent and says: "We could imagine that he was put into that position as chemist but was not really the chlorine gas maker or its initiator."

Deborah: "What Karen is saying, is that he might have been a placeman and not the real…"

John interrupts her and says:

"Imaginable. Some unknown German military chemists and scientists who had to remain anonymous, set him to be the producer of the gas."

George and Monica who had been following these utterances, and looking at all of these three speakers, look at one another and George says:

"Your attempts to convince us, haven't passed me, (he looks at his sister and continues), or my sister by unnoticed, so what is it to be?"

John: "How about a family journey? Karen and I, the parents, Monica and George, our children and you dear Deborah, the grandmother!"

Deborah: "Switzerland is to be, by car, or train?"

All of them look at one another and George asks: "By train?"

All nod positively.

On the Train to Dover

Monica and George open the sliding door of the compartment, come in and sit next to others.

John looks at the siblings and then to the rash passing by of the landscape through the window whilst the sun is shining in.

John asks: "Would you recommend the dining car, it was where you come from, wasn't it?"

George nods positively.

John: "I like the train's communication through its constant hiss, clicking on rail joint and squealing. It wants one to reveal hidden thoughts and the secrets which are still awaiting their release.

The wheels sliding on the rails, the rails carrying and rolling them and yet, both not wanting to separate from one another."

Karen and Deborah look at each other and then at John, wondering about his monologue but do not put any questions to him.

George says: "Yes, the hides!" and looks at his sister.

John: "Good places!"

George: "Yes, for the secrets. Mostly the ones, not willingly wanting to be kept anywhere although they are everywhere."

Deborah: "How about feelings such as; it might have been better to have done differently?"

Monica looks at them and says: "Feelings, having and not having them, secrets, what are you two trying to…?"

George interrupts her and says: "They want to know if there are some father and son, or if I may add you hither to, a father and daughter affiliations left or if they ever existed."

Karen interrupts him and says: "Or any conflicts existed, of this regarding's. From the beginning, till to a certain age. You follow? It is helpful to recall the past that had led to the "Gas", and as we are looking for reasons behind why he, your father, did what he did."

George interrupts her and says: "You even said that he might have been held intentionally to be the responsible and play the placeman."

Monica: "It is too much of talking, too much of wasting time and energy to even think about the past let alone to reminisce…"

John: "Yes, you are right why looking for him, a dying man or already a dead man and put to him all these questions now or post mortem, perhaps?"

Deborah: "It might prevent the newly usage of chemical weapons anytime and anywhere."

George: "I can't imagine that anybody could be able to be everywhere at the same time to stop its usage."

Monica looks at George and says: "It is confusing at times."

Deborah looks at Monica and asks: "Have you something to add to your brother's?"

Karen changes the subject and says: "Let us forget all that for a moment and enjoy the landscape before it escapes us unseen."

John: "Yes and think of what is yet to come."

Monica looks at John and says: "There were many military uniforms I saw and a sort of frenetic, surrounded us, people coming and going, asking my father how far he had proceeded with project."

Karen asks: "The or A project?"

Monica thinks for a moment and answers: "The project!"

John: "Weren't you able to hear or see any papers about the project?"

George looks at Monica and says: "How is she to remember, after so many years, you would better stop this a; no longer a conversation, but an interrogation!"

John: "You are right George; we might be able to ask him personally."

George: "Personally?"

Deborah: "Yes, face to face."

Karen: "If we only knew where he might be, how we could find him?"

John: "He might be innocent after all. Don't you want to assure yourselves of his innocence?"

George and Monica look at one another and remain silent for a while.

Shortly afterwards the train conductor slides the compartment's door to open, fronts his head into the compartment and announces: "Dover in 30 minutes!", looks

at George and says: "Your telegram was sent successfully."
He pulls his head back and slides the door to close.

John, Karen, and Deborah look at one another, John asks George:

"Should we know about the content of it?"

George: "Yes, I contacted a friend in Dover to join us, a close friend. He might have our father's last address."

Dover Railway Station

George: "This would be a short stop."

John: "We have to hurry to catch the ferry to cross for Calais and a train to Basel."

George: "There he is, next to the newspaper booth, I can see him."

They all go towards the news booth. George talk to him, the nods positively, gives George a piece of paper.

George introduces the man with the name of: "Edmund Franz."

They all leave the station for the ferry's landing dock.

On the Ferry to Calais

The sun is shining on the deck where they are sitting on the benches. Edmund Franz stands up and goes to smoke a cigarette on the upper deck. He is standing next to a protection barrier. A woman comes closer to him, shows him a cigarette in her hand. Edmund reaches for his lighter in his pocket, takes it out and lights her cigarette.

She thanks him and steps slowly away from him. Edmund turns back and looks to the see as suddenly he is being pushed down over the barrier and falls into the see.

The others who have been sitting on the bench stand up and stretch their legs as they hear voice from the upper deck screaming for help, shouting: "A man overboard!"

Astound and speechlessly, they look at one another to see if everybody is present.

John asks: "Where is Edmund Franz?"

Deborah: "Where did the shout come from?"

John: "From the balcony of the second deck. We must deny knowing him if we were to be asked."

George: "Whoever it was, must have known about him."

Monica: "You mean that he might have been murdered?"

John asks: "George, in the train, while you were sending that telegram…"

Monica interrupts him and continues: "Did you see anyone else except the train conductor?"

George: "No, but there was also a woman who was waiting to send a telegram."

Monica: "Could you see her?"

George: "No, she was with her back to me, but I think that she was an older woman."

John: "An older woman?"

Deborah looks at John and asks: "Henriette?"

John: "I know that she was released for an exchange of agents, you do not think that…?"

Karen: "She is working for the German Abwehr, again!"

John: "Once an agent, always an agent!"

Monica: "Who is this, Henriette?"

John: "A very old friendly enemy agent. Maybe she is doing it for what she lost."

George: "What did she lose?"

Deborah: "Almost everything except her life. I never met or saw her from afar."

John: "I wouldn't recognise her with certainty. I heard of her or probably saw photographs of hers. I don't remember to have met her. She must be in her 70s or 80s now, I suppose."

Monica: "You mean that we are being shadowed and do not know by whom?"

George: "By an assassin?"

Monica says anxiously: "It can be anybody on board."

Deborah: "There is no need to panic, do not turn around and looking for the pursuers. They are most probably unknown to us. We remain cautious, nevertheless!"

John: "Yes, it is better not to separate from one another till we reach France."

They reach the ferry landing place in Calais, and get off the ferry, get in a taxi and leave for railway station.

Railway station

They get on the train departing for Basel in Switzerland.

In the train Compartment

John: "He gave you something, a piece of paper or a note perhaps?"

George: "Yes."

Deborah: "Read it, please!"

George takes the note out of his jacket packet and reads: "Ingulie Str 2, apartment 6."

John: "Very well, we can look for that address, let me see if the train conductor has a map of Basel."

He leaves the compartment and looks for and finds the conductor in the corridor and asks: "Ich suche diese addresse in Basel. (I am looking for this address in Basel.)"

Conductor is looking at him and says: "I heard you speaking English with each other. I understand English. I am sorry but I do not have a map of Basel, but I know how you can get to this address."

John is surprised and says: "Can you? Please, show me the way when we arrive in Basel."

Conductor: "I can do more, since my shift ends at the station, I can take you there. Are you alone or with others?"

John is now looking suspiciously at him for his being too cooperative, says: "That would be awfully nice of you. I tell the others," and smiles whilst the conductor is smiling at him and is leaving him.

John remains in the corridor. He is watching him leaving this wagon and follows him in the next one.

The conductor knocks on a compartment with the curtains drawn down. He gets closer to the compartment's door to listen to what is being spoken. He hears a voice of a woman, a man and the one of the conductors, but he doesn't hear enough to understand what they are saying to one another.

John goes back to others and says: "We would be taken there by the conductor."

Karen: "The conductor?"

He looks at her and answers: "Unbelievably helpful. let's stretch out our legs outside, Karen!"

Karen stands up silently and leaves the compartment while the others remain sitting.

Outside of the compartment, John almost whispering, says: "The conductor was cooperative, actually, too cooperative, to offer his service to us, so I followed him into the next wagon. He went into a compartment totally shrouded. I tried to listen what they were saying to one another, but I couldn't hear properly.

I think Henriette should be in this train, in that compartment, and another man whose voice was older but familiar. I couldn't place him."

She says: "We would let the conductor bring us to that address."

John: "I hope that the address is the right one. And, how about the ones in that compartment?"

Karen: "Forget about them. We will be probably forced to encounter them later. But now we must find the chemist, and if not, some more clues from the conductor?"

John: "You are asking me?"

Karen haggs and kisses him and tries to calm him. They go back into the compartment.

John asks George: "You saw someone else besides the old woman?"

George thinks a while and nods negatively.

John looks at Karen and says: "That man, he might have been informed to be on this train."

Monica worrisome asks: "Which man?"

Karen: "An accomplice."

George closes himself to her, hugs her and asks:

"Which accomplice are you talking about?"

Monica: "It is confusing."

Karen looks at John and says: "You two, would better know that Henriette and another man who is unknown to us, are also in this train."

George and Monica looking to each other, Monica asks:

"What now? Let us go to them and finish this masquerade of hide and seek…"

George joins her and says: "Yes." He stands up and wants to leave, John holds him and tries to calm him. George starts to hit John with his fists. John hits him unconscious.

Monica asks: "What have you done to him, John?"

John remains silent and doesn't answer.

Deborah: "I guess we will be taken to that address, won't we?" She looks at John and John answers: "Yes."

Railway Station Basel

Upon arrival they have to wait till the conductor can join them. After half an hour, he joins them, and they get into two taxis and leave for that address.

During the drive, John asks the conductor: "I heard you talking to some people."

He answers: "Well, that is my job."

John: "Why are you offering your help to us strangers, and unknown to you? I don't see an enemy in you."

Conductor: "Your eyes seem to be intelligent."

John: "And?"

Conductor: "Be patient."

Ingulie Str 2, Apartment 6

They arrive at that address and get off the taxis. The conductor remains in one of the taxis and says to John:

"Go into that house, they are waiting for you."

John says: "We are unarmed."

Conductor: "So are they."

Deborah knocks on the door; an older woman opens the door and invites them in.

John asks: "Henriette?"

The older woman stops, turns her head towards them and answers: "Yes, John Barr, I am Henriette, sister of the chemist. He is awaiting his death. And you haven't given up your hunting for him, yet. There are also some other people here."

Deborah, John, and Karen are still standing in the corridor whilst someone's steps are getting closer to them.

The steps stop as a profile meets a ray of light through the skylight on the corridor's wall and lights it up. It turns towards them.

John: "Simon! You, here?"

Deborah and Karen are speechlessly looking at him whilst Simon answers: "Yes, follow me to the second floor."

During their climbing the stairs to the second floor, John asks: "Edmund Franz?"

Simon: "He was sent for you."

John: "To me? What for? By whom?"

Simon looks at him and does not answer.

John: "By whom?"

Simon: "Never mind that anymore. He could have been by any secret services."

John sees that Deborah is going closer to Henriette.

Meanwhile Deborah asks her:

"Why?"

Henriette is looking at her without answering.

John who is still looking at Deborah and Henriette, asks Simon: "Why should any secret service be interested in this plot?"

Simon: "For one reason to prevent us of dismantling the whole chemical weaponry. But I didn't have time to ask.

I gather, that they like the rest of the armies of the world, are profiting from the chemist's knowledge and what he might leave behind."

John: "Could George, the son I mean, know about that man's real identity?"

Simon: "No. That man was introduced to him before as the friend of the family."

John still watching Deborah and Henriette, sees that Henriette starts to speak to Deborah, saying: "How could have I told Samuel? At that time! I wanted to tell him in Hyde Park, but unfortunately, it was too late."

Deborah: "You could have halted your colleague, and you could have talked to your brother. I can imagine how sudden all that must have been, at that moment of his murdering. I cannot blame you."

Henriette reaches her hand to her, and Deborah takes it as they are climbing the stairs.

John remains silent and turns his head towards Simon as they reach the second floor, turn right in a big room with a bed in the middle of it, surrounded by oxygen cylinders with pipes joined to them.

One of them is connected with a pipe to a mask covering the face of a man lying in that bed. Besides the cylinders, there are a doctor, two German uniformed military men and three civilians.

They are talking with the doctor and looking at the man in bed and then to the rest of the group with John.

After a while the doctor comes to Henriette and asks: "It can be any minute now. Who are…?"

Henriette says: "They are some older acquaintances of him."

John nods positively and goes closer to Simon, grabs him on his elbow and asks him: "What are you doing here and what is going on?"

Simon: "He is dying."

John: "I see that. And you came here to show your respect and condole his sister and if I may add his children, too?"

Simon looks at George and Monica and says: "You gathered the missing pieces of our endless missions' puzzles, I see!"

John: "No need to be psychotic at this moment, tell me!"

Simon: "Paul and I, found out about his place by an anonymous information, at that time, now of course, I know that it was sent by Henriette, and we were on our way here as

Paul suffered a fatal stroke, I took his body back to London to bury and after the funeral, I pursued with the help of Henriette. I found him here, dying. Can you imagine after all what we experienced in searching for him. We are standing here in front of his death. It is reaching out for him."

John realises that Simon has been under immense pressure, let go of his elbow and says: "I am sorry old friend."

Simon: "Let us close this file."

John: "You know I cannot."

Simon: "Stubborn as ever, don't you see, or don't you want to let him die?

John: "I guess not. We do not have any information about what might come instead."

Simon: "Instead of what?"

John: "I meant about his chemical warfare research, is there a network which we can look into and…?"

Simon interrupts him and says: "Just a moment, are you planning yet another mission?"

John: "No, but there are signs of another war to begin in Poland, spreading wider and the usage of the gas in new forms might set out its murdering path again. A possible warfare scenario."

Simon: "You are speculating and also exaggerating. Don't you think that we are too old for new adventures? Look at Deborah, at Karen, it is time to end this never-ending spiral, dear old friend."

John looks at him and nods positively. They both, look at the two German military who are speaking with the chemist at his bed who now turn around und look intensively at John, Simon, Deborah, and Karen.

They turn themselves back to the chemist and salute him militarily, turn around and leave the room.

The doctor comes to John and Simon and says: "He wants to talk with you."

John: "With us?"

Doctor: "Yes."

John and Simon, astounded, go, and stand close to the bed. They hear a frail voice under the mask, trying to build some words that are now coming out of the mask, saying: "My sister had informed me before, about General Paul Slyer, at the very beginning of your chase for me. Is he also here?"

John: "No, he died. If you knew about his commando seeking you, and Henriette was trying to put you both in contact with one another, why then…?"

The chemist interrupts him and says: "I was under constant watch and was not allowed to have any contacts with anybody. Henriette told me just a little about you, a while ago. Even, then, during my experiments and production of the "Chlorine Gas", because of the surveillance having put on me, she couldn't come and talk to me about anything, never mind your attempts to convince me.

John: "My name is John Barr, and this is Simon Joyful. We were under his command. You seem to be losing your battle against eternity. Have you also let loose of your poisonousness essences?"

The chemist: "I didn't have much of a life, on the contrary as you know by now. I guess it wouldn't make any difference, if I were to say that I am sorry for what I produced."
Simon: "No, it is never too late to say sorry! But can you stop the poisonous machinery from further rolling?"

The chemist: "It is not and was not really under my control. It was there, the "Gas", I mean. It appeared on its own. I pumped it into a cylinder, the rest was and still is under military's decision making."

John looks at Simon and remains silent.

Simon: "How is the future to be?"

The chemist: "I don't know. I am leaving the future. You cannot foresee the future without understanding the past.

The circumstances we had to live under and what we had to give only to have an easier life."

The chemist continues: "It is out of my hands; it is an affair of the state. But the effects of it, have diminished.

All armies can launch countermeasures. Furthermore, it is becoming the most expensive.

Neither can I give you a guarantee for the prohibition of it nor for the usage of it in different and new forms by anyone, anywhere.

Don't forget; it is also out of your hands as it has been from the very beginning. We have to live with it."

John: "I am hearing the same words again."

Simon: "Now, I am hearing them, too."

The doctor comes to the bed and ask them to go back to Henriette who is standing by Karen and Deborah.

Deborah: "It seems to be a watch for his death and for the end of chemical warfare?"

Karen: "Are they separable?"

Henriette: "They were never joined to one another."

John and Simon look at them and nod positively, whilst they are witnessing doctor's closing chemist's eyes, the doctor's drawing of the sheet over the chemist's head and thereafter, doctor's announcing his death.

Monica and George remain standing silently by his bed whilst John, Deborah, Simon, and Karen are looking at them.

The End

62